Ruby Rogers'
In Your Dreams

Ruby Rogers
In Your Dreams

Sue Limb

Illustrations by Bernice Lum

BLOOMSBURY

First published in Great Britain in 2008 by Bloomsbury Publishing Plc
36 Soho Square, London, WID 3QY

Text copyright © Sue Limb 2008
Illustrations copyright © Bernice Lum 2008
The moral rights of the author and illustrator have been asserted

A CIP catalogue record of this book is available from the British Library

ISBN 978 0 7475 9244 0

All papers used by Bloomsbury Publishing are natural, recyclable
products made from wood grown in well-managed forests.
The manufacturing processes conform to the environmental
regulations of the country of origin.

Printed in Great Britain by Clays Ltd, St Ives Plc

1 3 5 7 9 10 8 6 4 2

www.suelimbbooks.co.uk
www.bloomsbury.com

CHAPTER 1
It's so NOT FAIR!

'IT'S SO NOT FAIR!' I was furious. 'It's completely and utterly totally mean and horrid!' I clenched my fists. I clenched my fists till they hurt. Everybody else at the table stopped eating. Mum looked surprised and cross. Dad looked nervous. Joe started to cook up a nasty smile. He loves it when I'm in a rage.

'Listen, Ruby, sweetheart,' said Mum, putting down her knife and fork. 'We explained a while ago that . . .'

'But it's not FAIR!' I yelled. 'I know what you're

going to say but it's not FAIR!!! Dan has a dog. Hannah has two dogs. Yasmin has a cat. And Lauren has cows and sheep and pigs and dogs *and* a cat! And a pony!'

'Yes, but Lauren lives on a farm, love,' said Mum. Her soft Welsh voice was beginning to sound a bit edgy.

'I agree,' said Joe with a mocking look on his face. 'It's not fair. I want a cow and I want it now. With mustard, ketchup and chips.' He did an evil grin at his own stupid joke.

'Look,' said Mum. 'You know Lauren's family are ever so fond of you. Her little brothers and sisters adore you. They said you'd be welcome to go there any time. Why don't you ask if you can go this weekend? There are still baby lambs being born every day, I expect. That would be nice, wouldn't it, love?'

'I don't want to have to go to Lauren's every time I want to cuddle an animal!' I snapped. 'I want to have one right here in our house. I want a pet. Everybody else has a pet! It's *so* not fair!'

'OK, listen, Rube.' Dad had finished his curry. He put down his knife and fork and took a sip of water. 'I know this is partly my fault, but I just want to remind you what would happen if we brought a cat in here. My eyes would start to itch. I would start sneezing. I would start wheezing and weeping. It wouldn't be a pretty sight. Do you want to subject your poor old dad to such torture?'

'Dad can't help having a cat allergy, Ruby,' said Mum, softening her voice. 'It makes him feel so ill. Remember what happened at that B&B in Devon?'

Remember it? Would I ever manage to forget it? We'd been driving back from the seaside one year and decided to break our journey at a guesthouse called Harbour View. Within a few minutes of entering the house, Dad's eyes had started watering. He sneezed. He wheezed. His face went bright red. Tears ran down his cheeks as if he was crying or something. It was *so* embarrassing; I tried to look as if I was adopted.

Apparently at Harbour View they had a long-haired cat called Mr Sardine. He wasn't even in the house at the time. He was snoozing on the garden wall.

But cats have this dusty stuff in their fur, called dander or something. I always imagine it's a bit like dandruff. Anyway, little bits of it drop off wherever they go, and it only needs a tiny bit of dander to get up Dad's nose to transform him from a perfectly normal geography teacher into some kind of

pink, pulsating, stand-back-everybody snot-and-tears machine.

We had to leave Harbour View right away, and ever since, wherever we go, we've had to ask if they have cats. Even if somebody had a cat six months ago and then the cat ran away or something, Dad's nose can still react to tiny bits of six-month-old dander.

Some dads can pilot jumbo jets. Some dads can climb mountains. Some dads can play football for Manchester United. Some dads are film directors in Hollywood. Or movie stars. Or architects. Some dads are prime ministers or presidents or kings and things. Or Formula-One racing drivers.

But my dad is allergic to cats. Weeping and wheezing is what he's good at. I do sometimes think that fate has dealt me a rotten hand.

'A dog, then!' I demanded. Dad isn't allergic to dogs.

Mum sighed.

'We've told you before, Ruby,' she said in a slow, clear voice as if I was an idiot or something. 'It's just not fair for a dog to be left alone in a house all day. Dogs should be out in the fresh air, running about. Think of Lauren's dogs. They're out with her dad all day, rounding up sheep.'

I thought of Lauren's dogs, Peggy and Tina. Peggy is black and Tina is grey. Peggy is crazy and clumsy and wonderfully intelligent, and Tina is older and a little bit snooty. Whenever I go to Lauren's farm they run up to greet me, wagging their tails. Even snooty Tina gives me a wag and asks for a little cuddle.

'If we had a dog,' I pleaded, 'I would take it out for a massive walk every morning before school. Then when I got home from school I'd take it out for another huge walk.'

'Oh yeah?' laughed Mum. 'Pull the other one, love! We can barely get you to school on time as it is – we're always in such a rush.'

'We could leave the dog out in the garden,' I said. 'Then it would get plenty of fresh air.'

'Dogs left in gardens bark all day long,' said Mum, pulling a face. 'We'd soon have the neighbours complaining.'

'Anyway,' said Dad. 'It's cruel to leave dogs on their own all day. They're sociable animals. In the wild, they live in packs. I know because in a previous life I was a dog. A wild dingo in the outback of Australia. I still get flashbacks. My name was Jason the Hairy. If we left the dog alone all day, it would howl.'

'And when dogs howl,' said Mum. 'They're really crying, love.'

'Think of the tears pouring down its lovable old snout,' said Joe. 'Rather like Dad in the middle of an allergy attack.'

I thumped Joe. This was supposed to be a serious discussion and, as usual, Joe was only interested in stupid jokes.

'Stop it, Ruby!' snapped Mum. Joe thumped me back, twice as hard. 'Stop it, Joe!' shouted Mum. 'Tell them to stop it, Brian!' She turned to Dad. Dad pulled a trying-to-be angry face.

'Stop it,' he said. 'Or there will be no pizza on Saturday night.'

Once in a blue moon (i.e. almost never), Dad can let rip and be really shouty. But he has to be in an absolute fury. Sort of hysterical. Mum's much better at being slightly cross in an everyday sort of way. Most of the time Dad gets us to behave by a mixture of threats and bribery.

I sometimes wonder what sort of teacher he is – I mean, if he's one of the nice friendly ones or the ferocious sort. He teaches in the next town, so we don't often meet kids from his school.

Just occasionally we might bump into one of his pupils when we go down to the Mall, just off the motorway. That's partly why Dad hates coming shopping – apart from his general hatred of shopping. Now and then he's forced to come because he needs new clothes or some kind of gadget. When we do see students of his, they usually just say, 'Hi, Mr Rogers!' and look embarrassed or start to giggle. I suppose teachers are minor celebrities in a funny kind of way.

'OK,' said Mum. 'Help me clear away the dishes, please, Ruby.' Joe got up and slouched off to his room, and Dad went off out to the garden. He's been mending the greenhouse recently and sowing lots of seeds.

'Another thing that's not fair,' I said, carrying

out the dirty dishes. 'Dad and Joe hardly ever help with the chores.'

Mum looked exasperated.

'I know,' she said.

'It's not fair,' I grumbled, pulling out the dishwasher basket, 'because you work just as hard as Dad.'

'I know,' said Mum with a rather bitter sigh.

'Well, it's *not fair*,' I said in a fierce, grumpy voice. Then I had an idea. 'Wait, Mum!' I yelled. 'I know! Why don't you give up your job? Then you could be at home all day and just relax, and then we could have a dog, because you could look after it and take it for walks all the time and keep it company and stop it from being lonely!'

Mum stood stock-still in the middle of the kitchen, placed her hands on her hips and glared at me.

'Ruby,' she said solemnly. 'I'm a midwife, OK? That's what I do. I've always wanted to do it, ever since I was a little girl like you. I deliver babies and it's a wonderful, wonderful job. It gives me a lot of satisfaction, plus it pays half of all our bills. If I gave up my job to look after this blessed dog, we wouldn't even be able to afford to live here any more. Is that what you want?'

'Yes!' I said rebelliously. 'Give up your job! I don't mind if we live in a log cabin, just so long as we can have a dog!'

Mum gave me a very sarcastic look and started to load the dishwasher.

It was like talking to a brick wall. However, I was determined. I made a secret, private and mysterious vow to myself, right there and then, as I slotted Joe's dinner plate into the dishwasher: I was going to get a pet, not just one day, when I was grown up or whatever, but *right now*, whatever my family said. I was going to have a pet by the end of next week. At the latest.

CHAPTER 2
Quick! Tell me! Tell me!

I DID GET AN INVITE to Lauren's house for tea on Saturday. Ever since Lauren first came to our school a few weeks ago, she asks me over all the time. I always love it. Well, I always have so far. But this time I felt in a funny kind of mood.

'Well, if it's an animal fix you want, now's your chance,' said Dad chirpily as we turned up the long muddy lane that leads to Lauren's farm. 'Sheep, cows, pigs . . . What else have they got here? Giraffes?'

I didn't laugh. Dad can be quite silly sometimes.

'Dogs, cats and a pony,' I said in a sighing sort of voice. I was looking forward to having a ride on Charlie the pony. Lauren's so lucky. She can have a ride on him any time. He's *her* pony. I didn't even have a pet spider.

Just as we drove into Lauren's yard, it started to rain. My heart sank. I knew I wouldn't be able to go for a ride on the pony now.

'Horrible rain!' I snapped, unfastening my seat-belt.

'March winds and April showers,' said Dad in a stupid sing-song voice, 'bring forth Pete Bowers.' Pete Bowers is a friend of Dad's who runs a garden centre. I had a feeling Dad was planning to drive off there afterwards and get some more seeds, or some new tools to keep in the shed. How boring! I hope you don't *have* to be interested in garden-ing when you're old.

I got out of the car and ran through the rain to the kitchen door. It opened as I arrived, and Lauren's little brothers peeped out.

'It's Wooby!' yelled Roly. I had to smile. Even though I was feeling quite fed up, little Roly always makes me laugh. He stretched his chubby arms up to me and I bent down and kissed him on the nose. Then I tickled his neck. He giggled and hid his face in his arms. It was almost like having a pet. If you could get furry babies, I bet they'd sell like wildfire.

'Hi, Ruby!' said Lauren. 'What a shame about the rain! I was all set to saddle up Charlie for you!'

Lauren's kitchen was cosy. Her mum was pouring a cake mixture into a tin.

'Mum's baking,' said Lauren with a happy smile. 'We can overdose on chocolate cake later. Hey! Come and see Rosebud.'

'Rosebud?' What new animal had Lauren got now? A camel, perhaps? A lobster? Some kind of exotic rat?

'She's a lamb,' said Lauren. 'She was born in the night and she got a little bit chilled, so Dad brought her in here to warm up.'

She led me to a box by the Aga. Inside was a tiny lamb, fast asleep. Her wool was thick and curly. I know all lambs are cute, but this one could have won an Oscar for Best Supporting Sheep.

'It looks as if she's got curly hair,' I said, stroking her little top-knot. She woke up and stretched.

'She's a Welsh breed,' said Lauren. 'Their wool is always like that.' She picked Rosebud up out of her box and put her down on the kitchen floor. Rosebud started pottering around on her little black hooves. They sounded like high-heeled shoes, clattering on the tiles.

'Gosh, you're so lucky,' I sighed, 'having all these animals. My parents said I can't have a pet. It's so unfair.'

'Here,' said Lauren. 'Give Rosebud a cuddle.' She picked her up again and handed her to me. I held her close. I could feel her little heart beating very fast. Her wool smelt nice.

'I wish she could be my own pet!' I sighed. 'Rosebud Rogers. It even sounds right.'

Lauren turned to her mother.

'Mum . . . ' she asked. 'Could Ruby take Rosebud home and keep her as a pet?'

Lauren's mum was wiping down the kitchen table. She pushed back her hair. You could see she was trying to think of a kind way to say no.

'I'm sorry, Ruby,' she sighed, 'but Rosebud has to go back to her mum later tonight.'

'But couldn't Ruby feed her with a bottle?' asked Lauren. It was really nice of her to speak up for me, but I sort of knew it would be no use.

'Not really,' said her mum. 'Rosebud isn't a pet, you know, love. She's going to grow up into a great big fat smelly sheep. She needs to live with a flock of other sheep or she won't be happy. And what would Ruby's mum say when Rosebud started to pee and poo all over her best carpet?'

Lauren sighed. 'Sorry, Ruby,' she said. She squeezed my hand. 'But you can come here whenever you like and see all our animals – can't she, Mum?'

'Of course!' said her mum with a smile.

'I wish I lived here,' I said. 'My family are rubbish.'

'Oh, that's not true!' said Lauren's mum. 'You mustn't talk about your family like that, Ruby.' I felt awkward. It seemed as if she was telling me off just moments after the friendly smile. 'Your family are so talented!' she went on. 'You should be proud of them.'

'I'm not proud of them,' I said bitterly. I knew I shouldn't argue with Lauren's mum but I couldn't help it. I had felt really cross for ages now. I was still angry from the family row yesterday. 'I'm totally fed up. It's because Mum goes to work that we can't have a pet. I wish she was like you.'

'Oh, I wouldn't wish this on anybody!' said Lauren's mum with a laugh. But it wasn't a totally happy laugh. It was one of those rather bitter laughs. She'd finished clearing away all the mess of the baking, she'd wiped the table down and now she was rinsing out the sponge. She sort of glared at the sink.

'In a minute I have to feed the hens and collect the eggs. Then I have to fill in three horrible forms. Then there are all the bills to pay and the records to keep. And Lauren's dad will be back from the farmers' market in a minute – and he'll be shattered and frozen and bad tempered and hungry. And all I really want to do is illustrate children's books! When do I ever get a spare moment to do that?'

She sounded really grumpy, even though she was still smiling. It was definitely one of those sarcastic smiles. I hadn't realised Lauren's mum had to do all those chores. And I had no idea she wanted to illustrate children's books.

'Can I see your drawings sometime, please?' I asked. This time her smile was real.

'Oh, how kind of you to ask, Ruby! Of course you can − if I can find them under the piles of junk mail from the Ministry.'

Just then Roly stumbled over, bumped his head on the table leg and burst into tears, and Lauren's mum picked him up and cuddled him, and shortly afterwards the door flew open and Lauren's dad trudged in and threw himself down in a chair.

'Call this spring?' he snapped. 'There was a wind coming down that alley today; cut us to shreds it did, sharp as a knife. What's for tea?'

Lauren and I went into the sitting room and watched a DVD of *Shrek*. I adore *Shrek*. My favourite character is the donkey. I wish I could have a donkey.

After *Shrek* we had tea (the chocolate cake was fantastic) but it was still raining, so I had to put on hold my plans to see the pigs and cows and everything.

'Never mind,' said Lauren, 'we'll play snakes and ladders.' We did . . . She won. I couldn't concentrate. I was thinking how wonderful it would be to have a pet snake. I would call it SSSSSSussssssan.

Eventually Dad came to pick me up. I might

have been in a sort of irritable mood all afternoon, but it was still hard to leave. I loved Lauren's house. Even when it was raining, there were two dogs and two cats and today there had been Rosebud.

'Did you have a good time?' asked Dad.

'Yeah,' I nodded. 'Lauren is so lucky, living on a farm.'

'Well, I've been thinking about this pet thing,' said Dad. 'And there's somebody special waiting for you at home, so do us all a favour and stop this infernal moping.'

My heart gave a gigantic leap. What? *What?* *WHAT???*

'Someone special?' I gasped. 'Dad! What do you mean? Tell me! Tell me!'

But he wouldn't say another word. All the way home, I was so excited I almost ate my own coat.

CHAPTER 3
Getting warmer!

WHEN WE GOT HOME I jumped out of the car and raced up the path. Dad followed, laughing.

'Easy, tiger!' he said, unlocking the front door.

'Where is it? What is it?' I gabbled, jumping up and down. Somehow I was imagining a little puppy curled up in a basket. In the kitchen, like at Lauren's house.

'He's waiting for you in the sitting room,' said Dad.

He, I thought. *It's a he!* My heart was beating

so fast I could feel my skin throbbing. I raced into the sitting room and looked around. Joe was watching TV. That was all.

'Where is he?' I yelled. 'Where's my pet?'

'I'm your pet,' grinned Joe. He rolled over on to his back, lolling his tongue out of his mouth and panting.

'Don't be stupid, Joe!' I snapped. 'It's not Joe, is it, Dad?' Dad was standing behind me in the doorway. He was grinning.

'No, no,' said Dad happily. 'He's much smaller than Joe, and he's covered in fur, and he's got a shiny black nose.'

'A puppy!' I screamed in joy. 'Where is he?'

'He's in this room somewhere,' said Dad. 'See if you can find him.'

Hide and seek with a puppy? It sounded weird. I looked all around the floor. Where else would a puppy be? I looked behind the sofa, and I ran round the other chairs. I looked behind the curtains. There wasn't a puppy anywhere. I mean, if you go into a room where there's a puppy, you see it straightaway, don't you?

I stood still in the middle of the room. I was baffled.

'Dad!' I said, puzzled. 'How can a puppy be in

here?' Mum had joined Dad. She was standing by the door, looking at me. But although Dad was still grinning in a stupid way, Mum looked uneasy. She glanced from me to Dad and back again.

'Brian!' she murmured in her special warning voice. She didn't say any more. It was odd. She seemed a bit cross with Dad or something.

'I'll tell you when you're getting warm,' said Dad, still enjoying the joke. If it *was* a joke. 'You know you always love that game.'

I took a step towards Joe, away from Dad.

'Getting warmer!' he said. I took another step. 'Getting warmer.' Maybe Joe had the puppy in his pocket or something. But you wouldn't roll over like Joe had just done if you had a puppy in your pocket, would you? You'd be extra, extra careful.

I went on moving across the room, step by step, getting warmer all the time. Right past Joe and onwards. I ended up in the corner where the home office is.

'Red hot,' grinned Dad. I looked at the floor. No puppy. I even peeped round behind the PC. No puppy. The screensaver was on. Then, suddenly, something appeared on the screen, along the bottom. A virtual dog! The puppy who advertises loo

rolls on TV! He strolled across and disappeared again. I stared at the screen.

'Absolutely boiling,' said Dad. But I didn't feel boiling at all. I felt as if I'd plunged into ice-cold water. I was sick with disappointment. I started to shake.

'It's a TV ad,' I said. 'Not a pet.'

'I told you, Brian,' said Mum softly.

'You can play all sorts of games with him,' said Dad. He came across the room now and sat down at the PC. 'Look – you can make him play with paint, you can brush him, you can tickle him – look at the menu.'

I turned away and strode coldly out of the

room. All the excitement of the last few minutes, all the thrill, the wonderful anticipation, had sort of curdled inside me and I felt as if I was going to cry or be sick. I brushed past Mum. She grabbed my hand and said, 'Wait, Ruby love . . .' But I pulled my arm away and ran upstairs.

I plunged into my bedroom and slammed the door. Then a huge explosion of tears burst out. I couldn't even climb up my ladder and cry up in my tree-house bed with my monkeys. I just lay on the floor and sobbed and roared and shuddered.

Soon I heard my door open and Mum knelt down beside me. I could smell her perfume. It was a special spicy one called Mitsouko that Dad had given her for St Valentine's Day. She put her hand gently on my back.

'Don't cry, Ruby, love,' she said softly. 'That was a stupid idea of Dad's and I've told him off. But he was only trying to help.'

'H-h-help?' I cried. 'Help? Making me th-think there was a real puppy waiting for me, a-a-and then, just to see that nothing – n-n-n-not a proper real live puppy at all. Just a-a-a TV ad! For loo roll!'

'I know, sweetheart, I know,' said Mum, stroking me. 'I'm so sorry. I'll make some of your favourite

cheesy potato for supper. Please stop crying. I hate to see you upset.'

I had more or less finished the main part of the cry anyway. I was into that shuddering and gasping bit afterwards. I decided to get up off the floor. The carpet was making my face itch. I got up and walked to my ladder.

'Come downstairs with me,' said Mum. 'You can help me make the cheesy potato and have extra little nibbles of grated cheese.'

'Don't want to,' I said, climbing up the ladder. I didn't want to go downstairs. Dad would be down there. I didn't want to see him at the moment. Or Joe. I reached the top and crawled into my bed platform.

'All right, then, that's right, have a little cuddle
with your monkeys,' said Mum. 'You've always got
your lovely monkeys, haven't you? They're better
than any pets could be, aren't they? And if you
look after them properly, they can stay with you
for all of your life. Till you're a very, very old lady.'

For once I didn't want to talk about my monkeys. I lay and stared at the wall. The monkeys
were up there: Funky and Stinker and Hewitt. But
they were just lying still. I didn't want to cuddle
them. Horrible feelings were still crackling and
flaring inside me, like a bonfire.

Mum had said my monkeys were better than
pets. But they weren't. They were different. You
couldn't compare them. I didn't want to argue
with her. I didn't want to be forced to say some-

thing about the monkeys not being real like pets, not being alive, because I didn't want to offend them. I didn't want to hear myself saying it either. I didn't want to offend myself.

And what she'd said about the monkeys lasting all my life was sad, too. Because what she was saying was that cats and dogs get old and die. I had another little cry about that. A tear ran sideways across my nose and into the pillow. I didn't make a sound, though. I didn't want Mum trying to climb up into my tree-house bed. She was still standing by the door, looking up at me.

'All right then, Ruby love?' she called. 'I'm really sorry about that, sweetheart. OK?' I didn't reply. I just lay there. 'I'll call you when supper's ready, OK?' I didn't answer. I heard Mum sigh. Then she opened the door and went out. She closed the door quietly, as if I was ill or something.

It was no use her apologising. She'd known Dad was going to play that awful, awful trick. Why hadn't she stopped him? I'd never been so disappointed in my life. My family was total rubbish. I began to make plans to run away – after supper.

CHAPTER 4

Help! Get it out! Get it out!

'SORRY MY IDEA kind of misfired, Rube,' said Dad as I sat down for supper. I gave a heroic shrug. I didn't smile. 'I realise now that it was a no-brainer. After supper I'll go and sit on the stupid step – if that's what you want?' He was trying to be perky, trying to make a joke of it.

'Oh, do shut up about it, Brian,' said Mum, dishing up the cheesy potato thing. 'Least said, soonest mended, isn't it? Beans, Ruby? And fried tomatoes?'

'Yes, please,' I said, still not smiling. They weren't going to get round me that easily. Joe kind of leant across the table and cocked his head on one side, right in my face.

'Small Girl Loses Rag in Tragic Virtual Pup Fiasco,' he said in his newspaper headline voice.

I very carefully didn't react at all. I pretended he didn't exist. Joe loves to get under my skin. He adores making me lose my temper. But this time I just wasn't going to.

'Could you pass the ketchup, please, Mum?' I asked. Mum passed it. I could see she was on edge. But I was getting Brownie points for not losing my temper. Mum usually grumbles if I cover my supper with ketchup. This time she didn't say a word.

'So . . .' she said, looking round with a determined smile as she picked up her own knife and fork, 'when are you going to put the new shed up, Dad?'

So Dad had a new shed, did he? How very dull.

'I'll start tomorrow,' Dad said. 'Perhaps Joe would like to help me.'

'Perhaps not,' said Joe.

'Maybe Ruby would like to help you a bit, eh, Dad?' Mum smiled at me. She was trying to make us be friends again. But it wasn't going to be that easy.

'No, thanks,' I said. 'The last time I helped Dad with something he hit me with a hammer.'

'Only slightly,' said Dad hurriedly. 'And you did move your hand just at the wrong moment. And it was an accident. And anyway, you made me hit myself with a hammer once – when you made me jump that time. So we're quits.'

'Maybe the new shed could be Ruby's pet,' said Joe. 'She could call it a name. Towser or Bonzo or something.' I ignored this as well.

'Don't be silly, Joe,' said Mum. Then she sighed. You could tell she was wishing that, instead of marrying Dad and giving birth to an idiot boy and

34

a small but sulky girl, she could have become a champion ballroom dancer or possibly emigrated to breed poodles in Hawaii.

'So,' said Mum. 'What's the weather forecast for tomorrow?' That was it. She'd given up all attempts to have a proper conversation, let alone a fun evening, and was now talking about the weather. At this point I switched off and began thinking about monkeys.

I've always liked the sound of South America and there are some very good monkeys there. I'd read all about them in a great book I got for my birthday. Their monkeys are flat-nosed, which is nice, and there are loads of different species. Some I'd really like to see are the capuchin (or organ grinder) monkeys, howler, spider, woolly and woolly spider monkeys, bald-headed uakari monkeys, squirrel monkeys and night monkeys.

All of these have a prehensile tail, which means they can use it like an extra arm or leg to grab things. But the South American monkey I'd most like to see is the pygmy marmoset. It's the smallest monkey in the world. It's about thirteen centimetres long with a twenty-centimetre tail. You could hold one in your hand just like one of Yasmin's Sindy dolls. Amazing!

I decided I would run away to South America in the morning – weather permitting. No way was I going to run away in the rain. But if it was fine and sunny, I'd dress up as a boy (i.e. my usual), empty my money box and stow away on a ship bound for Brazil.

My main problem was going to be finding a bag big enough to get Stinker, Funky and Hewitt into and leaving the house without arousing suspicion. I couldn't run away without them. Although I wondered what would happen when we arrived in Brazil and I introduced them to the pygmy marmosets. On the one hand, they would probably freak the marmosets out. On the other hand, the marmosets might freak them out.

'Ruby!' Mum's voice broke into my daydream. 'I said, *Would you like some apple pie?*'

I sat up and tried to look dignified but not particularly friendly.

'Yes, please,' I said. I wondered if they had apple pie in the Brazilian rainforest.

'Ice cream, cream, custard or yogurt?' asked Mum.

'Ice cream, please,' I said.

It tasted really delicious, but I tried not to look as if I was enjoying it very much. What I was really enjoying was sulking. There's nothing like a good sulk to pay people back for a horrid trick.

I sulked quite nicely on the sofa for a while after supper. Dad tried to snuggle up to me but I got up and pretended I wanted to go to the loo. Then, when it was time for bed, I kissed Dad goodnight, but it was an icy little kiss. My kiss for Mum was a bit better but it would only have scored four out of ten in a Kissing Competition (horrid thought!).

Needless to say, I didn't kiss Joe. I don't remember ever kissing Joe, actually. Sometimes Yasmin says, 'You're so lucky having a brother!' I don't think she realises what a complete pain it is. Ninety-five per cent of the time he is just worse than useless.

I went grandly up the stairs, undressed, did all the bathroom stuff, and then I got into bed and started playing with my monkeys. Funky is very bendy and sometimes I make him eat his own feet. It made me laugh.

Whoops! My sulk was wearing a bit thin. I had to try and keep it going, though, because the thought of those pygmy marmosets waiting for me in the rainforest was really cute.

I dozed off to sleep, hoping to dream of monkeys, but it was only the usual rubbish about going to school in my underwear.

Next morning I felt a bit lazy. I was still definitely going to run away, but obviously I was going
to have a nice cooked breakfast first. Dad told a
funny story about a man who got locked in a lavatory and I forgot I was supposed to be sulking and
laughed.

'Right,' said Dad. 'I'm going out to have a look
at my new shed.'

'He'll never manage to put it up without hurt-
ing himself,' said Mum, looking worried. 'Go out
and help him, Joe, there's a love – just for ten minutes. It's all come in sections, in panels – it just
needs putting together.'

Joe gave a horrid, blood-curdling, ghastly, long,
choking kind of groan, like someone whose skin is
being pulled off. He got up from the table as if his
body weighed about three tonnes, and kind of
heaved himself to the door.

I finished the last of my toast, then I decided I
would go out into the garden too. Of course, I was
still going to run away, but first I thought I would
just have a very quick look at Dad's new shed.

It was even more boring than I'd imagined. It
was just lying on the concrete bit that Mum calls
the patio – in pieces. Our old shed is at the far end
of the garden. Dad was planning to put this new

shed nearer the house, so he could have electricity in it or something. He was standing by the pile of sections, looking at a diagram.

As I stared at the pieces of the new shed just lying there, suddenly there was a voice in my ear. Joe was standing right behind me.

'Since you want a pet, Ruby, here's one — and this time it's *really alive*!' he hissed. And he put something down my back. Ugh! It was something wet and cold and dirty and horrid! A worm! A worm! I screamed.

'AAAAAAAGH! Help! Get it out! Get it out!'

This would never have happened if I'd had the sense to go straight off to South America as planned.

CHAPTER 5
Great! Great!

DAD CAME OVER right away and helped me to get the worm out. Thank God it didn't get inside my knickers. It was bad enough having it inside my vest. Joe just cracked up and ran off down the garden towards the old shed.

'Right, there you are, Rube,' said Dad, holding up the worm. It was quite a big one, and it was curling itself about in a kind of panicky frenzy.

'Ugh, ugh, ugh!' I screamed. 'Take it away! Take it away – but don't kill it!' I expect the worm was thinking something similar.

'Are you sure you don't want it for a pet?' said Dad, grinning. 'A worm called Wanda?'

'Shut up!' I shouted. That was it. Instead of comforting me and telling Joe off, Dad was joining in the joke. All Males Are Horrid Beasts. I made my mind up there and then to leave for South America immediately. In fact, I was heading for the back door and planning which shoes to take when suddenly Mum appeared.

'Yasmin's mum is on the phone,' she beamed, as if it was a special treat arranged by Mum herself. 'She's asking if you want to go over for lunch.'

'OK,' I said. 'But I'll have to change my vest first because Joe just put a worm down my back.'

'Ugh!' said Mum with a shudder. At last some sympathy. 'What a nasty trick!'

I went upstairs and found a clean vest while Mum made the arrangements on the phone with Yasmin's mum. I told the monkeys we'd be leaving for South America later. They understood. It didn't really matter to them.

'Hey! No problem,' said Stinker. 'We're ready. Just say da word, we're on the blocks.'

Soon I was ready to go. Mum appeared in the doorway, putting on her jacket.

'I'll take you over there,' she said. 'I can get some

milk on the way back. Why don't you take your monkeys with you, love?' Mum was trying to cheer me up again, but of course she got it totally wrong. I did take my monkeys to Yasmin's once and nobody realised how amazing they were.

Well, her big sister Zerrin did say, 'What cool monkeys, Ruby!' but that was it. Yasmin finds my monkeys boring. She'd rather dress dolls all day. Although Yasmin is my best mate, I have to steer her away from doll games all the time.

I hoped her mum would let us build a den. In summer we build dens in Yasmin's garden. It was probably a bit too cold to build a den outside today, but maybe we could build one indoors. Yasmin's mum is completely lovely and very understanding.

Mum drove me to Yasmin's. 'I wonder what you'll have for lunch, Ruby!' she said. 'Yasmin's mum is such a good cook, isn't she? I really envy her!'

This was true. Mum just isn't a brilliant cook at all, though she has mastered the basics and a few favourite things. However, when it comes to getting a baby out of a lady, she's the one to call. Not that it helps me very much. I'm never going to have any babies. Give me a pygmy marmoset any day.

'What did you have last time you came to Yasmin's?' asked Mum, making conversation like mad to prove that the tears and sulks were completely forgotten and in the past. I tried to remember the names of the delicious Turkish stuff I'd had at Yasmin's.

'Uh . . . hummus with pine nuts . . .'

'Lovely!'

'Sort of fried cheese with salad . . .'

'Mmmmm!'

'Chicken with a special sauce . . . walnut, I think she said.'

'Wow! I must get the recipe!'

'Oh, and last time I was there we had a lovely jelly. Pomegranate. It was a nice colour. Red.'

'Goodness, Ruby! Mrs Saffet should go on one of those celebrity chefs programmes, shouldn't she? She could teach them a thing or two!' laughed Mum as we reached Yasmin's house. 'I'm feeling really, really inferior!'

'Well, don't,' I told her as I got out of the car. 'That cheesy potato thing is my favourite.'

'Is it really? Oh, thank you, love!' said Mum, leaning forward for a goodbye kiss. I gave her a slightly more friendly kiss than last night's. This one would have scored about five out of ten. Or five and a half. Afterwards I slammed the car door

slightly too hard – just to show her I hadn't completely forgiven her for letting Dad play that mean trick on me. A virtual puppy! What complete rubbish!

The minute I walked into Yasmin's house everything seemed better. Yasmin gave me a huge hug. Zerrin gave me a huge hug. Yasmin's mum strolled over and gave me a little hug. Yasmin's mum is tall and wears floaty clothes. There was a wonderful smell of something cooking. A savoury cheesy tomato sort of smell.

'What would you like to do, Ruby?' asked Yasmin. This was polite of her. Usually she tells me what she wants to do right away. I suppose she was being polite because her mum was there.

'Could we make a den?' I asked.

Yasmin's eyes lit up. She turned to her mum.

'Oh, please can we, Mummy? Oh pleeeeeease!' She threw her arms around her mum (quite a feat – her mum is a big lady).

'Well, what I suggest is we have lunch first,' said Yasmin's mum. 'It'll be in about forty minutes. Then, afterwards, if you like, you can make a liddle den under the dinner table.' She says *liddle* a lot. It's the only time you can tell she grew up in Turkey.

'Great! Great!' screamed Yasmin. The table is quite big and we've made some fantastic dens under there in the past.

'We can pretend it's a nightclub,' said Yasmin. 'We can dress Tracey and Sophie and Angela and Fiona and Rachel up in their disco gear!' This was a reference to the dreaded dolls.

'Or . . .' I suggested, 'we could pretend we were camping in the South American jungle, on an expedition to study the pygmy marmosets. The dolls could be the marmosets.'

Yasmin looked suspicious.

'I don't like camping,' she said. 'Because of the creepy crawlies.'

'I will kill all the creepy crawlies,' I promised.

47

'You can be my husband,' said Yasmin. 'I will call you Jim.'

'OK,' I said with a secret sigh. It's quite hard being Yasmin's husband in a pretend way for just half an hour. I feel really sorry for the poor guy who's going to have to cope with her for the whole of his life.

'I still prefer the nightclub idea,' said Yasmin stubbornly, sticking her lower lip out a bit. Her future husband's going to have to watch that lip like a hawk. It's a sign of her mood.

'You could have a nightclub in the rainforest,' suggested Zerrin, who was slicing cucumber. I thought this was the nastiest thing Zerrin had ever said. She's usually the nicest girl in the world. But the idea of a horrid noisy nightclub in the forest? How would the poor monkeys get any sleep?

'Never mind about that, now,' said Mrs Saffet. 'Yasmin, why don't you take Ruby next door to see Mrs Fisher's new kittens?'

CHAPTER 6
Are you mad?

'**K**ITTENS?' I SCREAMED.

'Yes, they're *adorable*!' said Yasmin. 'I've already cuddled them five times.'

'Oh my gawd!' I yelled. 'You lucky *thing*! It's so not fair! You've got a cat of your own as well!'

'Otto isn't much fun,' said Yasmin. 'He's never going to have kittens anyway, because, first of all, he's a male and, second of all, he's been neutered. All he does is sleep all day.'

'Be careful crossing the road,' said Yasmin's mum. 'Look both ways.'

'Yeah, yeah!' shouted Yasmin, grabbing her jacket. We went out. The sun was shining and spring flowers were blooming in Yasmin's front garden. We looked about seven times each way before crossing the road, just to keep Yasmin's mum happy (and to stay alive, of course) and knocked on Mrs Fisher's door.

My past experience of Mrs Fisher is not brilliant. She has a whiney toddler called Jasper and a smelly baby called Cleopatra, and when it comes to money, she's as tight as anything. However, I was prepared to forgive her all this awfulness if she'd let us see the kittens.

The door opened, and Mrs Fisher smiled at us. Jasper was clinging to her leg as usual, and Cleopatra was asleep on her shoulder.

'Hi, Yasmin!' she smiled.

'Hello, Mrs Fisher!' said Yasmin in her polite voice. 'Could Ruby see the kittens, please?'

'Oh, hello, Ruby,' said Mrs Fisher. 'You helped Yasmin to clean my car once, didn't you?' I smiled and nodded, even though what she'd said was a lie. It had been my idea totally to wash cars for money. So if anything, Yasmin had been helping me.

'It was for charity, wasn't it?' said Mrs Fisher,

frowning and trying to remember. 'How did you get on? How much did you make? What charity was it again?'

I was already trembling with excitement at the thought of seeing the kittens, so it was really annoying of Mrs Fisher to start asking questions about something that happened so long ago.

'Oxfam,' I said. Yasmin gave me a look. She knew it was a lie. We'd really been collecting for my tree-house fund, and we'd only made a miserable twenty-five pence each. 'We had to stop after your car, though, because Yasmin didn't want to do it any more.'

'I expect my car put you off, ha ha!' said Mrs Fisher. 'It's always filthy! Look at it now!'

Mrs Fisher was so irritating. Who wanted to look at her dirty old car when she had kittens to see? Obediently we looked at her car. It was filthy. So what? She seemed to think having a filthy car proved what a wacky and wonderful person she was.

'You can do it again some time if you like,' said Mrs Fisher. How irritating could a person be? I'd just *told* her that Yasmin didn't want to wash cars any more.

'Maybe not today,' I said. 'It's a bit cold.'

'Maybe in the summer,' said Yasmin.

'OK, well, you'd better come in,' said Mrs Fisher.

At last! We nipped inside and that's when the smell hit us.

'Sorry it smells a bit,' grinned Mrs Fisher. 'But what with five kittens and Jasper and Cleo peeing and pooing freerange, it gets a bit like a farm in here sometimes.'

I didn't say anything but I knew it was nothing like a farm, because I'd been to Lauren's and the smell of farms is completely different. OK, there is a slight whiff of dung in the mix, but there's also hay and straw and engine oil and so many wonderful things. And the smell stays *outdoors*. Mrs Fisher's house just smelt like a lavatory.

'They're in the utility room,' said Mrs Fisher, even though Yasmin knew the way and was already almost there. I followed, holding my breath with excitement.

There, in the corner, was a box – and inside the box was a mother cat and her five kittens! She seemed to be lying with her front paws around them as if she was hugging them. It was a wonderful sight. Totally, totally cute.

'Aaaaaaahhhhhhh!' we said in unison. The toddler Jasper lurched towards the box.

'No, Jasper!' said Mrs Fisher, pulling him away. 'He doesn't really understand how to handle them,

yet. But you can pick them up – you've touched them before, haven't you, Yasmin? Be very gentle.'

The kittens were all different colours: black, white, brown, mixed and grey. It was the grey one I fancied. He was very fluffy. His fur stood out all round his face like a kind of saucer – a bit like a pygmy marmoset.

'Can I hold the grey one?' I asked.

'He's called Horatio,' said Mrs Fisher. Yasmin picked him up carefully and handed him to me. He was absolutely beautiful. My heart melted. My hair practically turned pink with sheer joy. I was in love.

A shame about the silly name, though. Mrs Fisher obviously had a mad streak when it came to choosing names. Imagine a baby called Cleopatra, for a start.

'What are the other ones called?' I asked, stroking Horatio's velvety fluff.

'The mother's Bianca,' said Mrs Fisher. 'The little brown-and-white girl is called Sabrina, the black and white is Giorgio, the black with white tips is Cassandra, and the stripy one is Newcastle United.'

'Amazing names!' I murmured. Horatio was now trying to climb up the front of my jumper. His little claws were like tiny needles.

'I've always overdone it a bit when it comes to names,' said Mrs Fisher. 'Possibly because I'm called Ann and I've always been bored by it. My husband named the Newcastle United one, obviously.'

Secretly I thought that naming cats after football teams was a much better idea than all that fancy Italian stuff. If I had Horatio – if he was my kitten – I would call him something else. I wasn't sure what, yet.

'He likes you, Ruby,' said Mrs Fisher, smiling. Horatio had got as far as my shoulder.

'He's adorable!' I sighed. 'I wish I could have one. How much are they?'

'Oh, they're free to good homes,' said Mrs Fisher. 'They're not pedigree cats or anything,

although I think the father must have had a bit of Persian in him. That's why Horatio and Giorgio are so fluffy.'

'When will they be old enough to leave their mother?' I asked. A really, really naughty but wonderful idea had sprung into my mind. My heart started to race.

'Oh, another week or so should do it,' said Mrs Fisher.

'I want Horatio!' I suddenly burst out. 'He's utterly fabulous! I love him to pieces!'

'Really, Ruby? You'll have to ask your parents, obviously.'

'Yes, yes, of course,' I said. 'I'll ask them and let you know.' Yasmin was giving me a puzzled look. She knows all about my dad's cat allergy. I gave her a special hard kind of glare, a warning not to mention it. She understood.

We went on playing with the kittens for a while and then it was time to go.

'Ten minutes is about right for them to be handled at the moment,' said Mrs Fisher. 'They still need a lot of time with their mother. But by the end of next week they should be ready to go to their new homes. So let me know, Ruby – if you really think you might be able to take Horatio.'

'Yes, of course,' I said, giving him a last cuddle before I put him back in the box with his mum. We stood up.

'Thank you very much for letting us see the kittens,' said Yasmin in her polite voice.

'It was a pleasure,' said Mrs Fisher graciously. Unfortunately, a moment later Cleopatra was sick all down her shoulder. It was only white milky baby sick, but all the same, it certainly speeded our exit.

'Are you mad?' said Yasmin as we crossed the road (after looking both ways fourteen times, of course). 'I thought your dad had a cat allergy?'

'It's not as bad as it used to be,' I said. 'I think they might have cured it. I'll find a way to get Horatio. But listen, Yas . . . Please don't say anything about it to anybody at the moment, OK?'

'OK,' said Yasmin. Her eyes were huge. 'I promise.'

CHAPTER 7

Not too near! Not too near!

'SO HOW WAS lunch at Yasmin's?' beamed Mum as I arrived in the kitchen.

'Oh, great, thanks.'

'Did you say thank you to Mrs Saffet?'

'Yeah, yeah.'

Dad was doing a crossword at the kitchen table. He looked up and pulled a funny kind of face, as if he'd forgotten something.

'What did you have?' asked Mum.

'Oh, something like a sort of macaroni pie thing.' I wasn't really listening. I was already planning where in the house I could hide a real live kitten without anybody noticing.

'Aah – ahh – ahhh . . .' Dad was going to sneeze. He always makes a great big performance of it. 'Ahhh – CRACKATOA!!'

'Brian!' exclaimed Mum. 'Are you getting a cold?'

'Aaaah – no, I think it's . . .' Dad got up and went over to the kitchen roll. 'Aaaah – ahh – ahh – OOOJAMAFLIP!' Dad often says silly words when he's sneezing. He tore a piece of paper off the roll and blew his nose.

'I think it's a cat hair situation,' he said, looking at me accusingly.

'Oh dear,' I said. 'I did stroke Yasmin's cat a bit.'

'Aaaah – aaah – aaah – WHACKADEGULLION!' roared Dad. His eyes were starting to water. 'Take that girl away from me!' he said, backing off to the other end of the kitchen and flapping the piece of kitchen roll at me as if I was a wasp or something.

'Ruby!' said Mum, handing me a carrier bag, 'Upstairs, please. Change all your clothes, put the dirty ones in here and bring them down to me. They'll go straight in the washing machine, and you'll go straight in the shower.'

Hmmmm. As I went upstairs I could hear Mum

getting the vacuum cleaner revved up and whizzing it across the kitchen floor – just in case any bits of cat dander had dropped off me or something.

I changed my clothes and took them down to Mum. Then I went back upstairs and had a bath and shower. I lay in the bath and had a think. How was I going to keep Horatio secret? And before that, how was I going to pretend to Mrs Fisher that my parents had said yes to a kitten? And where was the soap?

However, no matter how difficult it all was, I certainly hadn't given up my wicked plan. I was going to have Horatio as my very own kitten, somehow.

I had sort of been thinking, as Yasmin's mum drove me home, that I might *just* mention the kitten idea at home, just to sort of test the water sort of thing. Dad's outburst of mad sneezing had put paid to that idea right away.

As for pretending that I'd got permission, that might not be too tricky. I could write a letter to Mrs Fisher on the computer, saying it was OK for Ruby to have a kitten, and forge my mum's signature on it. Most of the letter would be printed anyway so it wouldn't matter if the signature was

a bit wild. Anyway – Mrs Fisher had never seen Mum's signature, had she? She didn't even know her. So it wouldn't matter if I didn't get the forgery part quite right.

I was slightly relieved when I realised this. The main problem, though, was to find somewhere in the house where I could keep a kitten without anybody noticing. I had to go and look at my bedroom again. I got out of the bath, dried myself and washed the bath out (extra points for saintliness, and you have to be thorough with allergies).

Then I shut myself in my room. The only possibility was the wardrobe. I could see that right away. I opened it. There was a lot of rubbish in the bottom of it, but if I cleared it all out there would be plenty of room for a little box with straw or something. And a cat litter tray. Hmm. I hoped it wouldn't stink too much.

'What ya doin?' enquired Stinker. I looked up. He was lying on the edge of the bed platform, looking down at me. Briefly I explained the situation. Maybe Stinker would have some ideas. He was, after all, a gangster as well as a monkey.

'Hmmm . . . Don't like the sound of that cat,' he mused thoughtfully. 'Don't want a newcomer movin' in on my patch.'

It seemed nobody was on my side, but I was still determined. At least I would forge the letter to Mrs Fisher. First I had to wait until nobody was in the sitting room, so I could use the PC without being seen.

I went downstairs. Mum had finished vacuuming and was ironing in the kitchen. Joe seemed to be out. He's usually out on Sundays.

Rather inconveniently, Dad was watching a gardening programme on TV. The PC is in the corner. I had to get him out of there. I stood by the sofa and had a quick think.

'Not too near! Not too near!' cried Dad in alarm,

slithering away from me. 'You come in here coated with allergens and drape yourself all over me!'

'I've had a bath and washed my hair and changed my clothes and everything,' I said.

'Well . . . OK then,' said Dad doubtfully, looking at me as if I had the plague or something.

'How did you get on with the new shed?' I asked. 'Can I see it?' I knew if I could tempt him out into the garden he'd probably stay there till it was dark.

'I haven't done very much yet,' he admitted. 'I need to do a bit of concreting first.'

'Can you show me, Dad?' I asked, trying to sound cute and affectionate. He hauled himself to his feet and switched the TV off. 'I think I could be quite interested in gardening when I grow up,' I said, taking his hand and looking up adoringly like a lovable puppy. Or indeed kitten.

'Let's have a look, then,' said Dad. We went out into the garden. It was a total mess. Bags of cement and sand lay everywhere, and the panels of the new shed were still lying in a heap. It was about as boring and nasty as our garden has ever been.

'It's going to be lovely,' I said. It was hard to think of something positive to say.

'I suppose I ought to do a bit more,' sighed Dad.

I wondered if it was too soon for me to go back indoors again. Then I had a brilliant idea.

'Shall I bring you a cup of tea out here?' I asked. Dad cheered up slightly.

'Oh, yes – thanks, Rube, that would be nice,' he said. 'I should really get on with this concreting before it gets dark.'

I ran indoors and went straight to the PC. We have a document all ready which has our address on, so I only had to write a few lines. It went like this:

Dear Mrs Fisher,
    Ruby has told me about the kitten

Horatio. It would be OK for us to have him. Thanks very much. I will send Ruby around to collect him next week.
Yours sincerely, Mrs Rogers.

I quickly printed it off, signed it in a scribble, grabbed an envelope, sealed it safely inside and wrote *Mrs Fisher* on the front in big letters.

All I had to do now was give it to Yasmin at school tomorrow, and ask her to deliver it for me. The permission side of things was sorted. Horatio was as good as mine. But where was I going to hide him?

CHAPTER 8
Oh my God!
What's the matter?

NEXT DAY AT SCHOOL everything was hunky dory. Knowing I was going to have a kitten seemed to give me lots of extra energy. I even got full marks in a spelling test. And Yasmin promised to deliver my letter to Mrs Fisher.

'Is it really OK for you to have Horatio, Ruby?' she asked.

'Yes,' I said with a little secret shiver of guilt. I don't like lying to Yasmin, but I wasn't sure if she'd deliver the letter if she knew I'd forged it.

'So have your mum and dad changed their minds about you having a pet, then?' said Yasmin.

'Yeah . . .' I tried to sound casual. 'They're cool about it.'

'But what about your dad's cat allergy?'

'Oh . . .' I hesitated. 'Dad's taking some pills or something that gets rid of it.'

'How brilliant!' Yasmin clapped her hands in quite a charming way. 'Pills are ace!'

She ran off happily with my letter, but I didn't feel completely relaxed about it as I climbed into Mum's car. In fact, I was beginning to worry. What if Yasmin mentioned the kitten to her mum, and then her mum mentioned it to my mum? Our mums often meet and chat while they're waiting for us to come out of school. It would be the obvious thing to talk about.

Yasmin's mum would say, '*Oh, I hear you're having one of Mrs Fisher's kittens.*' And my mum would be, like, '*Whaaaaaaaaa?*' or something. My neck went kind of cold at the thought of it.

'What's wrong, Ruby?' said Mum. 'You look tired.'

'I'm fine, Mum!' I managed to switch on a bright but false smile. 'We had a spelling test today. I came joint top.'

'Well done, love!' said Mum.

'Did you have any nice babies today?' It's our daily joke.

'Yes, a nice little red-headed girl,' said Mum. 'Her mum was a fashion designer and she said, "Oh no! All the Babygros are pink! They'll clash with her hair!"'

I managed to laugh, but I couldn't really concentrate on the ginger baby. Secretly I was thinking about the kitten. Any minute now Yasmin would be putting the letter through Mrs Fisher's letterbox. And maybe she'd be telling her mum that my dad's cat allergy had been cured by pills.

It had been a big mistake to lie to Yasmin. I should have let Yasmin in on the secret and got her to help me do the lying. I'm so stupid. I'll never make a gangster.

Mum wanted to do some grocery shopping on the way home, so we went to the supermarket. I usually love going food shopping. I choose all my favourite stuff and try to smuggle it into the trolley. But this time I just couldn't face it. I was so worried about the kitten business, I felt kind of sick.

At last we got home. I was longing to run up to my room and shut myself in. I needed to talk this

over with the monkeys. I had a feeling I'd made a really big mistake and their advice is always useful. Well, Stinker's is. All Hewitt ever says is, 'Anyone for tennis?'

We arrived home, parked the car and carried in the shopping – three bags each. We dumped it in the kitchen and Mum started to unpack it.

'Dad!' she called in a cheery voice. 'Guess what! We've got lemon-curd-flavour yogurt! Come and get it!'

There was a kind of groan and a strange rustling sound from the sitting room. Then we heard Dad's voice, and it sounded weird.

'If only I could!' he called.

Mum frowned and pushed past me in a hurry.

'Brian?' she called. Then she went on: 'Oh my God! What's the matter?'

I ran in after her and what I saw made my heart lurch. Dad was lying on the floor, face down, with his head turned to one side, looking away from us.

'It's perfectly all right,' he said. 'It's just my back.'

'Oh, no!' said Mum. 'Not your back again!'

'Yes, just like that other time, when Ruby was a baby, remember?' groaned Dad. His voice sounded strained and ill.

'Well, what's set it off this time, then?' asked Mum, sitting down on the sofa and staring down at him.

'I think it was heaving that sack of cement about yesterday evening,' said Dad. 'I thought I felt something go then, and it's been getting worse and worse all day. I had to lie down on the staffroom floor at lunchtime to ease the pain.'

'Oh, Brian,' sighed Mum.

'How long will you have to lie like that for?' I asked. I felt really sick now. Seeing Dad lying there was awful. He looked half dead.

'Only about six weeks,' said Dad.

'What!?' I yelled.

'Dad's joking,' said Mum. But she didn't look very amused. 'He just has to lie like this for a day or two, then start to walk about as much as he can. Gently.'

She heaved another huge sigh and got up again.

'Is there anything I can get for you now?' she asked. She sounded almost fed up with Dad. It was awful. 'I assume you won't be able to go to school tomorrow?'

'No,' said Dad. 'After my performance on the staffroom carpet today I don't think they'll be expecting me.'

'Well, is there anything we can do to make you more comfortable, Brian?' asked Mum.

'I'm still interested in the possibility of dinner,' said Dad. 'Only I'll have to eat it out of the dog's bowl.'

Dad couldn't stop joking, even though his face was really pale and he was in so much pain. If only we had a dog, it could keep him company on the floor.

'Don't stand there looking down at me like that, Ruby,' said Dad. 'You look like somebody watching a snake. I know I look bizarre but I'm quite OK. Go and help Mum.'

I went back to the kitchen. Mum was unpacking the groceries. She looked cross.

'I told him to get a couple of chaps in to put that blinking shed up,' she said. 'But he wouldn't listen.'

'Well, he won't be able to argue now,' I said. 'Why don't you just ring them up and ask them to come and do it? Then, by the time Dad gets better, the shed will be ready and he can just enjoy it.'

'Great idea!' said Mum. 'Only I'm not quite sure who to ask. I don't know any builders or handymen ... I know! Maybe Yasmin's parents will know somebody. Her father always has workmen in to do things, doesn't he?'

I gulped. This was my worst nightmare. Mum was going to ring Yasmin's mum and within seconds Mrs Saffet might be saying, *'I'm so glad you can have one of Mrs Fisher's kittens'* . . .

I put some yogurts away in the fridge to hide my face. I was sure I was blushing and looking guilty.

'I don't think he's got a shed,' I said. 'I don't think he knows those sort of workmen. I could ask Yasmin tomorrow at school.'

'Oh, don't let's wait that long,' said Mum. 'I'm sick to death of this blinking shed business. Let's do it now.' And she grabbed the phone.

CHAPTER 9
Watch out! Danger!

I RAN OUT OF the back door and down to the bottom of the garden. My heart was hammering like mad. Right at the bottom of the garden is the old shed, and between the side of the shed and the back fence there's a small gap. I went in there and hid. My mind was racing. What would Mum say?

'What's all this nonsense about a kitten?'

And what would I say? Hundreds of excuses and explanations flew through my head so fast, I couldn't tell what they were. Then my mind slowed down to a crawl. Then it stopped completely and refused to come up with a single word.

But I had to work out my defence. *'Sorry, Mum, it was supposed to be a joke.'* Hmmm. That wouldn't work. Forging a letter from Mum and actually having it delivered to another grown-up? That was a major crime, let alone the kitten aspect of things.

'Mum, we can have a kitten, because I've heard of these pills that can cure a cat allergy.'

Then she'd say, *'What pills? Where did you hear about them?'*

'Mum, I'm sorry, I'm really sorry, but if you could see Horatio, you'd fall in love with him too.'

'Listen, Ruby! I'm far, far too busy to do all my usual things, let alone look after a kitten!'

'Mum, just let me explain: Horatio can stay in my bedroom. He can stay in my wardrobe.'

'Ruby, don't you understand? Your dad is allergic to cats! Having a kitten anywhere in the house is going to set him off! And besides, you can't keep a kitten in a wardrobe! It'd be cruel!'
In my mind, Mum had an answer for everything.

I felt utterly crushed. I leant my head against the side of the old shed. Birds were singing nearby. In fact, one of them was doing his alarm call:

'*chink, chink, chink!*' Dad taught me a few of the birdsongs once, but I wasn't really interested. But I remember what '*chink*' means: *Watch out! Danger!* Even the birds seemed to know that Mum was on the warpath.

Living with my family was so stressful. Although I'd more or less forgotten about my plan to run away to South America, right now I wished I was in somebody else's family. My mum was always stressed out. In my opinion, she'd be happier if she gave up being a midwife and worked at home like Yasmin's mum.

Yasmin's mum is always chilled out and smiley. She works as a translator in her little office upstairs, but she's always there if Yasmin needs anything, and she pops down to the kitchen all the time to put delicious things in the oven. I wished I could be adopted by Yasmin's family. I'd become a Muslim and everything, no problem. I think they're cool.

And Lauren's mum is always at home too. OK, she'd said she was rushed off her feet, trying to be a farmer's wife and do book illustrations. But she's always there to take care of Lauren and the little ones, and the cats and dogs. I wished I could be adopted by Lauren's family. That would be even better, because I could share the pony.

My family was rubbish. My mum was always racing around, trying to do too much, tired from her work, dozing off on the sofa, forgetting things. My dad was a hopeless wimp, always hitting himself with hammers and putting his back out and sneezing and crying if there were cats around.

Yasmin's dad is fierce and strong and manly and he's got an important moustache. If my dad tried to grow a moustache, it wouldn't be black and stylish. It would be weedy and drooping.

It was only a matter of time now before Mum threw the back door open and shouted, *'Ruby! Ruby!'* And then I'd get the telling-off of a lifetime. I sighed. I felt quite tempted to run away. But I was starting to feel hungry.

I was also quite tempted to have a cry. My chin actually twitched madly for a few moments. But I decided to fight it off.

I crept round to the front of the shed and peeped inside. It was full of junk and it was looking a bit shabby and rotten. But still – oh my gawd! Oh my gawd! The shed! *The old shed!*

Dad wouldn't need the old shed any more once he'd got his new shed put up, so I *could keep Horatio in there*! In the old shed! He could have a blanket and toys and everything! And he could come out into the garden when he wanted some fresh air! He needn't come into the house at all! I was sure Dad wouldn't react to the cat dander if Horatio stayed outdoors!

I ran back up the path, full of hope again. Mum was going to tell me off, but I had my answer. The old shed! It was perfect! I could even paint his name on the door: *Horatio's House*.

My new idea was fabulous, but I had to be careful now. I mustn't burst in and start yelling. It could ruin everything. I had to be subtle. I had to be clever. I opened the kitchen door quietly and slid inside. I was kind of cringing already in case

Mum had heard all about the kitten from Yasmin's mum. She might be hopping mad and ready to tell me off right away.

She was unpacking the groceries and she did look cross. I cringed a bit just to be on the safe side.

'Ruby!' she snapped. I jumped – not right out of my skin, but sort of halfway out. 'You were supposed to be helping me unpack the groceries!'

'OK, sorry,' I said, and started putting things in the lower cupboards right away to save Mum having to bend down. I waited for the storm of fury to break over my head. Any minute now she was going to raise the subject of Horatio. But she said nothing. However, she did look rather grim.

'I forgot the blinking toilet paper!' she said. 'Would you believe it?'

'It's OK,' I said, trying to soothe her. 'We can use tissues.'

I was surprised she hadn't mentioned the phone call to Yasmin's mum yet. I put the new cleaning stuff under the sink.

'This bad back of Dad's is a real nuisance!' she said. 'Last time he was in pain for weeks.'

'We can help him, though,' I said in angelic mode. 'We can look after him. You're a sort of nurse and I can bring him things. Will he be lying on the floor for many days, Mum?'

Suddenly I thought how embarrassing it would be if my friends came round. If Dad had to lie

still in pain, I wished he would do it upstairs out of the way. I didn't like him lying on the carpet like that, as if he was a dog or a cat. If I was in a Roald Dahl story, my dad would become my pet. Problem solved. But in real life, it was weird and annoying.

Mum still hadn't mentioned the kitten. She looked as if she was thinking about other things. I decided to do a little gentle probing.

'What about the new shed?' I asked. 'Did you get through to a workman?'

'Oh, no . . .' Mum looked as if that was just one other thing that was causing her stress. 'Yasmin's line was engaged – I tried three times. I'll ring them later. After supper. It's fish pie tonight.'

Normally the news that it was fish pie would fill me with horror, but right now I had other fish to fry. It seemed a perfect moment. Mum hadn't talked to Mrs Saffet after all. She didn't know about my letter to Mrs Fisher. Phew! I had to act fast.

'Mum,' I said. 'When Dad's got his new shed, what will happen to the old one?'

'Ruby,' said Mum, looking tired and edgy, 'I have so much on my mind. The fate of the old shed doesn't even begin to register on my radar.'

'Well, could we keep it for a while, then?'

'I suppose so. Dad will probably use it to store things. You know – his used plasters, his odd socks, old newspaper cuttings about potatoes looking like politicians, that sort of thing.' It's true that Dad does find it hard to throw things away, and it drives Mum up the wall.

I took my courage in both hands. Now was the moment. I had to say it.

'Mum,' I said. 'Couldn't we have a cat and keep it in the old shed? Then it would never have to bother Dad at all. Oh – per-leaase!'

CHAPTER 10
Oh, don't say that!

MUM'S FACE SORT OF turned to stone. Her eyes flashed. Her lower lip stuck out. She heaved a huge sigh – a really irritated, fed up, sarcastic sound. I cringed.

'For crying out loud, Ruby!' she yelled. 'How many times do I have to tell you? No, you CAN-NOT have a cat! Didn't you see how Dad reacted when you came home yesterday – just because you'd stroked a cat in someone else's house? Can you imagine how Dad would react if there was a cat out in the shed and you were sneaking out and cuddling it all day long? Do you want your dad to be sneezing and his eyes running all day long as well as lying on the floor? Do you not understand *plain English*?'

I should have just quickly said, 'S*orry, OK – forget I ever mentioned it*,' but somehow instead there was an explosion of rage inside me.

'It's so unfair!' I yelled. 'We can't ever have any pets because of your stupid job and Dad's stupid allergy! Lauren's got pets! Froggo's got pets! Yasmin's got pets! Everybody's got pets except us! I hate this family! I wish I'd been adopted! – No, I wish I'd never been born!'

'Ruby!' shouted Mum. 'Don't you ever, *ever* talk to me like that! That's a horrible, horrible thing to say! I've got enough on my plate without you behaving like a complete idiot! If you can't cooperate and be helpful, go to your room!'

I raced upstairs, thumping my feet really hard on each step. I flew into my room and slammed the door with the most almighty crash. Then I climbed up on to my bed platform and grabbed my secret diary and a pencil off the shelf by the bed.

I was shaking with rage. I found a clean page and let rip: *I hate Mum*, I wrote. *I hate Mum. I*

hate Mum. I wrote it over and over again, like a punishment, until the whole page was covered.

Then I felt kind of sick. I ripped the page out of my diary. I threw the pencil at the opposite wall.

'Hey!' gasped Stinker. 'Whass the problem? Whass goin' on round here?'

'If you want to cry,' said Funky, 'please, use my tail to wipe your eyes.'

I didn't want to cry, though. I was just furious. I lay and glared at the wall for hours. Until four o'clock. Then Mum called upstairs: 'Tea time!' I'd planned to stay up in my room, but by now I was starving. Being in a rage must burn up loads of calories.

I went downstairs. But I wasn't going to be nice. I sat down in my chair and glared at the table. Joe had come home, but thank goodness Tiffany wasn't with him. I don't hate her like I did at first. She is nice to me and stuff. I just didn't want any strangers to be there, so I'd have to be polite.

'Cheese on toast, Ruby?' asked Mum. She was using her cold, polite voice. Not her usual perky Welsh sing-song voice.

'Yes, please,' I replied, twice as cold.

'Young Girl Sulks for England, Shock Horror,' said Joe, shaking the ketchup bottle. 'Thousands Flee.' I ignored him.

'Cheer up, old bean,' said Dad. He'd got up off the floor, thank God, but he was sitting on the edge of his chair in a weird way, with his back very straight. 'You may not be able to have a cat, but I'll be your pet. You can feed me and teach me tricks.'

'And de-flea him,' said Joe. 'And take him for walks so he can pee against lamp-posts.'

'Joe!' snapped Mum. 'Don't be such a blinking idiot! And watch out – you'll knock your drink over in a minute.'

I managed to keep my cool and I didn't say a word for the rest of the meal. I didn't smile at Dad,

86

even though he tried his hardest to coax me into it. I didn't glare at Joe, even though he tormented me whenever he got the chance. I didn't even look at Mum. She was the worst mum in the world and she didn't deserve any more love at all.

My fury was still there next morning. I woke up furious. The first thing I saw was the piece of paper saying *I hate Mum* about a zillion times. I still meant every word of it. I didn't screw it up and throw it away. I just left it lying there on my bed.

I ate a furious breakfast and I went to school furious. I hated my family. I came bottom in a maths test. To be fair, that might have happened anyway.

At break Yasmin offered me one of her mum's divine cheese sandwiches. The cheese is always grated and the bread is so, so soft. This was the best moment for hours and hours, but it only confirmed my fury at my own useless family. If my mum tried to grate cheese, it would turn to worms, maggots and sand.

'Can I come to your house after school tonight?' I asked her.

'Oh, yes, Ruby!' grinned Yas. 'Fantastic! We can play the *X Factor* with my dolls.'

'OK,' I sighed. 'But first I have to go across the road and tell Mrs Fisher I can't have a kitten after all.'

'That's such a shame!' Yasmin cried. 'But maybe you can have a kitten when you're grown up?'

'When I'm grown up,' I told her, 'I'll have kittens wall to wall!'

I texted my dad to say I was going to Yasmin's. He texted back: *ENJOY*. But I was dreading it. What would Mrs Fisher say? She might be really cross.

Yasmin didn't come with me to see Mrs Fisher. I didn't want her to. I was still a bit ashamed that she thought my forged letter was really from my mum, when it wasn't. I told her I'd be back in a minute, looked right and left about sixteen times, and crossed the road.

Mrs Fisher's bell rang with a horrid shrill sound. My heart was beating like mad. Mrs Fisher was going to be really annoyed with me for changing my mind. And it was vital she didn't find out that I had forged that letter.

'Hello, Ruby!' she beamed, opening the door. For once she didn't have Cleopatra sleeping on her shoulder, but Jasper was standing beside her, clinging to her leg. 'Come in!'

As I stepped inside I smelt all Mrs Fisher's various odours, including the cat smell. But I didn't mind the stink. I felt really jealous that Mrs Fisher had all those kittens and we had none.

Jasper wasn't even old enough to know how to treat animals properly. Toddlers always pull their tails and torment them and stuff. As for Cleo, she didn't even know what a kitten was yet. These kittens were wasted on the Fishers.

'Where's Yasmin? Is she coming? Would you like to see Horatio? I got your mum's letter,' she said.

'No, I – er – I can't stay, really,' I said. 'I just came to say that we can't have Horatio after all. I'm really sorry.'

Mrs Fisher frowned.

'But your mother said –'

'It's just that my dad's got a cat allergy,' I said, starting to gabble as I began the lying business. 'We've only just found out. He's been sneezing and stuff, and we thought he had a cold, but it's a cat allergy.'

'Oh dear, I'm so sorry. What a shame,' said Mrs Fisher. 'Still, it can't be helped, I suppose. And to tell you the truth, I was beginning to feel a bit sad about parting with Horatio. He's such a poppet. I think, if you don't want him, we'll keep him ourselves.' And she looked rather pleased.

'You're so lucky,' I said. 'I wish I lived here. My family is total rubbish.'

'Oh, don't say that, Ruby!' said Mrs Fisher.

'No, I hate them,' I said, although as I said it I felt a horrible pang of guilt. 'My dad's useless with his allergy. And if my mum didn't go out to work, we could have a dog.'

'But it's quite a good thing in a way, your mum going out to work, isn't it?' said Mrs Fisher.

'No,' I said. 'She comes in late, we never get nice home-baked cakes like Lauren and Yasmin have, and she always falls asleep on the sofa when she gets home – instead of looking after us.'

'It sounds to me as if you should be looking after her!' said Mrs Fisher with rather a silly laugh. 'What does she do that leaves her so tired?'

'It's stupid,' I said. 'It's a really stupid job. She's a midwife.'

'A midwife?' Mrs Fisher looked really interested.

'But that's a wonderful job, Ruby! My midwife saved my life when Jasper was born.'

'Saved your life?' I was surprised.

'Oh yes,' she said. 'She was absolutely amazing. Rhiannon her name was. Rhiannon – something.'

What! Rhiannon was my mum's name! I suddenly felt myself sort of blush all over.

'My mum's called Rhiannon,' I said. Mrs Fisher looked intrigued.

'What's your surname again, Ruby?'

'Rogers.'

'That's it! Rhiannon Rogers! Your mum saved my life, Ruby – and what's more, she saved Jasper's life too. In my eyes, she's an absolute hero!'

CHAPTER 11
I've been thinking . . .

I WAS SO STUNNED, I left in a daze. I'd no idea my mum had ever saved anyone's life. Saving people's lives . . . well, I thought it would involve jumping into the sea or something. As I crossed the road back to Yasmin's (after looking left and right about seventeen hundred times) my arms and legs started to feel lighter. I sort of almost flew across.

Yasmin's mum was waiting, looking a bit anxious. Yasmin looked nervous too, as if they were expecting me to be crying or something. Mrs

Saffet put her arm around me. She's so lovely.

'Never mind, Ruby,' she said. 'Let's go and have some chocolate brownies – you'll soon feel better.'

'It's really tight that you can't have Horatio,' said Yasmin. 'After your mum said yes at first and everything.'

I thought I'd better keep quiet on that score.

After the brownies and juice, we went upstairs and played the *X Factor* with Yasmin's dolls. But my mind wasn't on the game. I kept thinking about that horrid hate letter I'd left lying on my bed: *I hate Mum. I hate Mum* ... Even now Mum could be reading it. It made me feel sick to think about it.

Yasmin was singing away in the character of Lara, her doll with the long blonde hair, in a specially bad wavery voice, which was supposed to make me laugh. I tried hard to look amused, but I couldn't manage more than a pretend smile.

'OK,' she said, after the song. 'And now, over to the judges.'

I was supposed to be the judges – all three of them. I used the deep growly part of my voice to sound like the men judges. Two of Yasmin's boy dolls were playing the parts.

'Look, Yasmin, sorry but I think I ought to go home,' I said. Yasmin looked crushed.

'At least do the judging for Lara!' she hissed. I went through with it – I mumbled and growled a few rude remarks, and then the Lara doll attacked the Simon judge doll and there was a big row. Yasmin loves that sort of thing. But I was desperate to escape. I struggled to my feet.

'Sorry, Yas,' I muttered. 'I gotta go.'

'But you've only just come!' said Yasmin.

'I need to get home . . . I was in a strop with Mum,' I explained. 'I want to make it up with her.'

'Ring her, then,' said Yas. But I didn't dare. The thought of Mum finding that *I hate Mum* thing was too awful. She doesn't often go up to my bed platform, but she does sometimes, when she changes the sheets. I wouldn't be able to say a word until I was sure she hadn't been up to my room.

We went downstairs and Yasmin asked her mum to drive me home. She was in the middle of frying some onions, so Mr Saffet said he'd take me. This was a bit frightening, but he didn't say a word on the way back: he just switched on the radio news and went '*tut, tut*' all the time at all the horrible things happening in the world.

'Thank you very much, Mr Saffet,' I said politely as I got out. He nearly smiled. I felt quite pleased that he'd nearly smiled at me. It was a bit of an achievement. Yasmin's dad is kind of scary.

But now I had to face the music. The *I hate Mum* essay. It was like a poison-pen letter. My tummy crumpled up at the thought of it. Why hadn't I thrown it away? Why had I just left it lying there?

I didn't go in through the front door. I went round the side to the garden – I thought I'd sneak in through the back. The garden still looked a total mess with the shed panels lying about and the concrete sacks spilling powder everywhere. I heard that bird alarm call again: '*chink, chink, chink*!' As if they were complaining about the state of the place.

The back door was open. I tiptoed into the kitchen: another fine mess. Dirty plates everywhere. No nice smells of cooking. Not like Yasmin's house or Lauren's house. I put my bag down and walked into the hall. There was the sound of the TV burbling away quietly in the sitting room. I peeped in through the open door. Mum was asleep on the sofa, with a coffee mug on the carpet beside her. There was still a little bit of coffee in it, but it had gone cold and cloudy.

She was lying on her back with her hands on her tummy. Her mouth was open and a little strand of spit was sort of strung between her top lip and her bottom lip, blowing to and fro every time she breathed. Her eyelashes were golden and curly. Her nose was covered with freckles.

I know those freckles very well. They're shaped a bit like those stars in the sky – The Plough, I think it's called. At the corners of Mum's eyes were little wrinkles – crow's feet. I could sort of see a bit what she'd look like when she got to be a really old lady.

I looked at her hands. The fingers were curled up, kind of like paws. She doesn't wear nail varnish. Her nails are cut short. I think it's to do with hygiene and being a nurse. Her fingers twitched slightly in her sleep. I thought how my mum's hands were different from any other hands I'd ever seen. If you showed me hundreds of photos of different pairs of hands, I could tell which were Mum's right away.

She sighed in her sleep – it was a faraway sort of sound, like the sea on a distant shore. This was my mum: asleep in a chaos of dirty dishes, tired out from saving people's lives.

I tiptoed out and ran upstairs very softly because I didn't want to wake her. My hateful hate

letter was lying just where I'd left it, on my bed. I immediately tore it into a hundred pieces, then carried the pieces to the bathroom and flushed them down the loo. Some of them wouldn't go down and I had to poke at them with the loo brush. I was so ashamed that I'd written something so vile. I put ordinary loo paper scrunched up on top and had to flush three times before every tiny fragment of the hate letter had gone.

'Ruby?' I heard Dad's voice call from the bedroom as I came out of the bathroom. I followed his voice. He was lying on the bed, on top of the duvet, with his clothes on, so he didn't look too horribly ill, thank goodness. He held out his hand. I sat down on the bed and gave him a kiss.

'Hi, Rube,' he said. 'How was school? Come home to care for your invalid parents?'

'How's your back, Dad?' I asked.

'Absolutely tickety-boo. I'm really just shamming,' he said. 'But the only thing that bothers me is that there's so much for your mum to do, now I'm useless. Give her a hand, will you? What's she doing?'

'Sleeping,' I said. 'Don't worry, Dad – I'll go and clear up.'

'*Not a child, an angel!*' said Dad in a funny,

high-pitched American voice, as if he was quoting from a film. I went downstairs and looked round the kitchen.

How typical of Joe to be out at a time like this. Boys are so useless. Joe hardly ever helps with anything.

I picked up the first dirty plate and started to load the dishwasher. I recycled all the left-over veggie peelings that were just lying in the sink. They went in the compost bucket.

I wiped down all the surfaces and rinsed the cloth. Then I swept the floor. I was just wondering if that would be enough, when Mum walked in,

yawning and stretching. When she saw the kitchen she stopped in her tracks. She looked amazed, and then a big smile broke across her freckly face.

'Oh, Ruby love, you've done wonders,' she said. I went over and hugged her. She smelt like she always does: it's like the smell of summer, but I don't know why.

I wouldn't tell her about Mrs Fisher and what she'd said about Mum saving her life. I'd save it up for another time. I didn't want to remind Mum about Mrs Fisher. She might want to go off and visit her or something, and then she might find out that I'd written the letter and pretended it was from her. It's terrible when you've done something wrong and you're trying to cover it up. The after-effects seem to last for ages.

'I'm so tired,' said Mum. 'I think it'll have to be fish and chips tonight. Still, it isn't very nutritious. You don't mind, do you, love? And Ruby . . . I've been thinking.' I looked up. I could see a tiny bogey roosting in her nose, but it didn't matter. 'I've been thinking . . . I know how upset you were yesterday, and I'm sorry, but I've had an idea that might, well, sort of make it up to you a bit.'

CHAPTER 12

Oh wow! This is the best day of my life!

I WAITED, PUZZLED. What could possibly make it up to me? Mum looked uneasy, sort of guilty-ish. What was coming?

'We could cope with . . . a tank of tropical fish,' she said. My heart sank. Here was Mum trying to be kind, but fish – honestly! I could hardly curl up on the sofa with a fish on my lap, could I? I could hardly play ball-of-string games with a fish. A fish couldn't sleep on my bed.

'It's OK, Mum,' I said. 'Thanks, but no thanks.

Fish just aren't fluffy enough.' Mum sighed. 'I couldn't cuddle them,' I sighed too. 'It's OK. I've got my monkeys.' Mum gave me a strange look. For a moment our eyes locked, and we kind of had a silent pact not to say anything more about the monkeys compared to kittens or whatever.

'Never mind, love,' she said again, and put her arm around my shoulders. 'I've had another idea.'

'What?'

'It's nothing to do with pets, I know, but when Dad's got the new shed up – he phoned some workmen today and they're coming next week, by the way – anyway, when he's all set up with his new shed, well . . . you could have the old shed, if you like. As a sort of den.'

She looked down at me with shiny eyes. I couldn't let her see how *not* excited I was. OK, a shed. A den if you like. Somewhere to play. But, to be honest, nowhere could be as good as my tree-house bed platform that I already had, indoors.

Besides, the shed was smelly and full of spiders. Yasmin would never agree to go in there. She'd run screaming from it. It was hardly a wonderful new thing to be proud of. But I had to pretend to Mum that I was thrilled.

'Brilliant, Mum! Thanks so much!' I grinned,

and threw my arms around her and hid my face, so she wouldn't see how really less than thrilled I was. 'I'll go out and have a look at it now!' I ran out of the kitchen and found myself in the garden.

For a moment I just stood there, getting used to being outdoors. It felt different. The air was fresh and breezy. That was good. There was the smell of earth, and some of the trees were covered in new green leaves.

I noticed the tulips had come out – Dad planted the tulips last autumn and told me that one day, in spring, I'd see something gorgeous. They were pink and purple and white – beautiful.

There were also some tulips called parrot tulips which Dad had told me about. Their petals were kind of curly and fringed, like a parrot's feathers. Maybe my parents would try and fob me off with the parrot tulips as pets! I grinned slightly at the thought. But it was a rather sarcastic grin.

I strolled down to the bottom of the garden. Birds were singing. In fact, they were doing their alarm call thing again: *'chink, chink, chink!'* Birds seem alarmed all the time. They're such scaredy-cats. Oh, I suppose that is literally what they are: scared of cats. So if I'd had Horatio and kept him down here in the shed, the birds would have been going *'chink, chink, chink'* all day and all night. Nightmare.

At the thought that I would never have Horatio, a tear ran out of the corner of my eye. My insides felt all heavy. I was glad to be friends with Mum again, and I was proud of her instead of fed up with her, but I was still really, *really* sad that I would never be able to have a kitten.

When I'm grown up I'm going to have fifty kittens at least. My castle on the coast of Wales will be full of them. I brushed the tear off my cheek and decided to have a look at the old shed. I knew it was full of Dad's old junk, but when he cleared it out there would be a bit of room. I could bring the monkeys here for a day out and we could have a picnic, even if it rained.

All the same, it was still a gloomy place and I felt gloomy as I peeped round the door. There were old pots of paint, packets of seeds, broken flowerpots and rusty tools scattered everywhere. Dad is so untidy. I sighed. It looked forlorn. I felt forlorn. Without a kitten, it was rubbish.

I stepped inside. The windows were cracked and dirty. It would take a miracle to transform this place into a desirable den. I looked up at the roof. There were one or two places where the wood had rotted. Holes in the roof. Worse and worse.

Then I heard a strange sound – *churrr!* – right in the shed, in front of me, in the heaps of rubbish. Suddenly I saw it, and my heart almost jumped right out of my mouth. There, in an old broken flowerpot, was a bird's nest – with five baby chicks looking up at me with their beady little eyes. *And they were about as cute and fluffy as anything has ever been!*

'Oh my gawd!' I gasped.

All the chicks opened their little yellow beaks at the same time, like a choir of beggars.

I staggered backwards. I knew it was important not to touch them, and to let their parents look

after them. I heard the *'chink, chink, chink'* sound
again, and as I stepped back outside the shed, a
robin flew in right past me, with some grubs in his
beak. He – or she – perched by the nest and fed
the babies right there and then, with me watching
and everything! Amaaaaaaaaazing!

I ran indoors.

'Mum! Dad!' I yelled. 'There's a nest in the shed!
With babies in it!' Dad had just arrived downstairs.
His back was still stiff, but at least he was walking
about. 'Come and see! Come on!' I shouted.

We tiptoed down the path. *'Chink, chink,
chink!'* came the alarm call.

'It's OK, Rob, we're not going to hurt your
babies,' said Dad. 'There he is – look, Ruby – on
that branch.' I looked. The adult robin was looking
at us.

'Robins are very tame,' said Mum. 'My dad used
to train them to eat out of his hand.'

'I bet we could easily do that,' said Dad. 'They're
always desperate when they're feeding their
young. Damned kids – always so demanding. Eh,
Ruby?' He gave me a little nudge.

'Poor things!' smiled Mum. 'Working their little
socks off to look after their babies. I'll get them
some bread.' She went indoors, and came out a

few minutes later with some crumbs. She threw them on the ground. The robin flew right down and pecked some up, even though we were only a couple of yards away.

'Oh, yes,' said Dad. 'He'll be eating out of my hand by tomorrow afternoon. And then, when you get home from school, you can have a robin perch on your head, eh, Ruby? Would you like that?'

My heart gave a crazy little leap.

'Could I?' I breathed. 'Really?'

'You bet,' said Dad. 'And then, when the young ones learn to fly, they'll be tame too. We'll have to keep an eye on them and chase all the cats away.'

'I'll do that!' I said, full of joy. 'I'll chase all the pesky cats right over the horizon! And maybe if the baby robins are very tame I can get them to come into my bedroom and perch in my tree house. Do you think they would, Dad?'

'Oh, certainly.'

'Would it be OK, Mum?'

'OK, then – but you'll be the one who has to clear up the poo.'

'OK, OK! I'll clear up every speck of it! Oh wow! This is the best day of my life!'

This was better than having a pet. This was

going to be having a wild thing that was also your friend. It was going to be marvellous. I had a new pal, and his name was nothing fancy like Horatio. His name was Robin Rogers.